A Note to Parents and Teachers

Kids can imagine, kids can laugh and kids can learn to read with this exciting new series of first readers. Each book in the Kids Can Read series has been especially written, illustrated and designed for beginning readers. Humorous, easy-to-read stories, appealing characters, and engaging illustrations make for books that kids will want to read over and over again.

To make selecting a book easy for kids, parents and teachers, the Kids Can Read series offers three levels based on different reading abilities:

Level 1: Kids Can Start to Read

Short stories, simple sentences, easy vocabulary, lots of repetition and visual clues for kids just beginning to read.

Level 2: Kids Can Read with Help

Longer stories, varied sentences, increased vocabulary, some repetition and visual clues for kids who have some reading skills, but may need a little help.

Level 3: Kids Can Read Alone

Longer, more complex stories and sentences, more challenging vocabulary, language play, minimal repetition and visual clues for kids who are reading by themselves.

With the Kids Can Read series, kids can enter a new and exciting world of reading!

Yummy Riddles

Marilyn Helmer

Eric Parker

Kids Can Press

For Sarah Elizabeth MacDonald – M.H.

Kids Can Read is a trademark of Kids Can Press

Text © 2003 Marilyn Helmer
Illustrations © 2003 Eric Parker

Kids Can Press acknowledges the financial support of the Ontario Arts Council, the Canada Council for the Arts and the Government of Canada, through the BPIDP, for our publishing activity.

Published in Canada by   Published in the U.S. by
Kids Can Press Ltd.   Kids Can Press Ltd.
29 Birch Avenue   2250 Military Road
Toronto, ON M4V 1E2   Tonawanda, NY 14150

www.kidscanpress.com

Edited by David MacDonald
Designed by Marie Bartholomew

Printed and bound in Hong Kong, China, by Book Art Inc., Toronto

The hardcover edition of this book is smyth sewn casebound.
The paperback edition of this book is limp sewn with a drawn-on cover.

CM 03   0 9 8 7 6 5 4 3 2
CM PA 03   0 9 8 7 6 5 4 3 2 1

National Library of Canada Cataloguing in Publication

Helmer, Marilyn
    Yummy riddles / Marilyn Helmer ; illustrator, Eric Parker.

(Kids Can read)
ISBN 1-55337-446-0 (bound).   ISBN 1-55337-412-6 (pbk.)

1. Riddles, Juvenile. I. Parker, Eric II. Title. III. Series: Kids Can read (Toronto, Ont.)

PN6371.5.H45 2003   jC818'.5402   C2002-902989-9

Kids Can Press is a *lorus*™ Entertainment company

What do you get if you drop a plate of pasta?

Splat-ghetti!

What is the best day of the week to eat ice cream?

Sundae

How do airline pilots cook their bacon
and eggs?

In flying pans

Why did the farmer plant seeds in his pond?

He was trying to grow watermelons.

What kind of nut has a hole in the middle?

A donut

What kind of drink do owls like best?

Hoot-beer

What did the girl rocket say to the boy rocket?

Let's go out to launch!

How did Santa Claus get around when he hurt his foot?

With a candy cane

What did the eggs do when the cook
wanted to make an omelet?

They scram-bled!

What is Dad's favorite treat at the movies?

Pop-corn

When is it okay to drink milk from a bowl?

When you're a cat

What looks like a half a tuna sandwich?

The other half

Which hand should you use to stir your hot chocolate?

Neither — use a spoon!

Knock, knock.

Who's there?

Olive.

Olive who?

Olive the pizza was gone before
I got a piece!

Which vegetable has toes but no feet?

Pota-toes, of course!

How many raisins can you eat on an empty stomach?

One – after that your stomach won't be empty.

What do lumberjacks take to the grocery store?

Chopping lists

If you dropped a turnip, a cabbage and a pumpkin on your foot, what would hurt the most?

Your foot

What did one pork chop say to the other?

Pleased to meat you!

What kind of cookies would you feed your pet canary?

Chocolate chirp cookies

What do cows put on their pancakes?

Lots of moo-ple syrup

Who saw Little Miss Muffet eating her curds and whey?

A spider spied her.

What kind of soup do teachers like best?

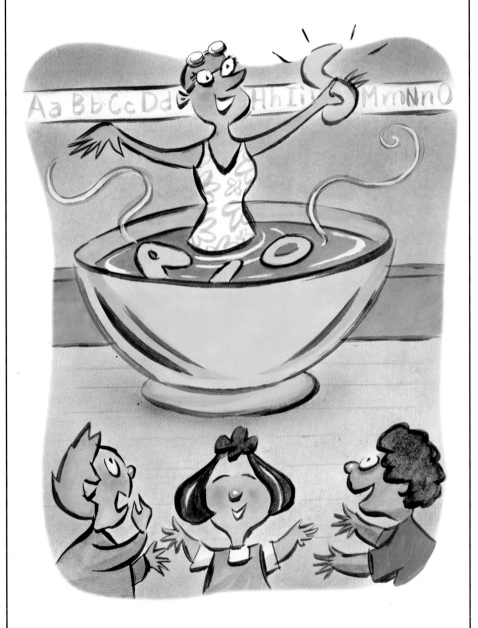

Alphabet soup

What did the french fry give his girlfriend when they got engaged?

An onion ring

What's cold and red and wears boxing gloves?

Fruit punch

What kind of candy would you give
someone in prison?

Jaily-beans

How do you make a strawberry shake?

Sneak up behind it and shout, "Boo!"

What do you have if you're holding seven apples in one hand and six in the other?

Very big hands!

What do you call a dinner that talks back to you?

Rude food

Knock, knock.

Who's there?

Bacon.

Bacon who?

Bacon my mother a birthday cake!